SCHOLASTIC

My First Little Readers

by Deborah Schecter

NEW YORK • TORONTO • LONDON • AUCKLAND • SYDNEY
MEXICO CITY • NEW DELHI • HONG KONG • BUENOS AIRES

Teaching *Resources*

*In memory
of Maggie*

Cover design by Maria Lilja

Interior design by Sydney Wright

Illustrations by Anne Kennedy
except pages 6 and 13 by James Graham Hale, and page 9 by Rusty Fletcher

ISBN: 0-439-57407-2
Copyright © 2004 by Deborah Schecter
Published by Scholastic Inc.
All rights reserved.
Printed in the U.S.A.

8 9 10   40   11 10 09 08

Contents

Introduction

Welcome to *My First Little Readers*, a collection of 25 little books written to correlate to Guided Reading Level A, and designed to support children at the emergent stage of reading. The stories feature a variety of familiar and favorite topics that children will enjoy reading about, such as preparing for the first day of school, playing with friends, the outdoor world, seasonal changes—and themselves! *My First Little Readers* will help children get a great start in reading as they learn to love to read!

My First Little Readers include the following features:

* Consistent text placement on each page
* One to two lines of text per page
* Short sentences with repetitive sentence structure
* Repeated and recognizable high-frequency sight words
* Rhyming text to build recognition of word families and other phonics skills
* Engaging illustrations that closely match the text
* Familiar story themes that connect to children's experiences and interests

Tips for Using *My First Little Readers*

Before Reading Take a picture walk through the book with children and invite them to tell what they think the book will be about, make connections to their own experiences, and identify familiar and unfamiliar words. Discuss strategies children can use to decode unfamiliar words, such as finding beginning or ending sounds, breaking the word into parts, and using picture clues. Provide background for any concepts in the book that might be unfamiliar to children.

During Reading Let children read the book aloud softly as you listen in. Help children use problem-solving strategies when they encounter unfamiliar words. You can offer support and encouragement without interrupting the flow of their reading.

To assess children's decoding skills, take a running record as they read, noting the problem-solving strategies used by each child as well as strengths and needs. Use these questions as a guide:

☑ Do children follow the print with their eyes (indicating greater fluency) or use their fingers to follow the words?

☑ Do they recognize most words or use their knowledge of sound-spelling relationships to decode unfamiliar ones?

☑ How well do children use context clues from surrounding words and pictures to figure out the meaning of new words?

☑ Do they self-correct by rereading to pronounce difficult words or to improve expression?

☑ Do children use appropriate inflections when they encounter question marks, and interpret other punctuation correctly?

How to Make the Little Readers

Follow these steps to copy and put together the mini-books:

1 Remove the mini-book pages along the perforated lines. Make a double-sided copy on 8 ½- by 11-inch paper.

2 Cut the page in half along the solid line.

3 Place page 2 behind the title page.

4 Fold the pages in half along the dotted line. Check to be sure that the pages are in the proper order, and then staple them together along the book's spine.

NOTE: If you cannot make double-sided copies, you can photocopy single-sided copies of each page, cut apart the mini-book pages, and stack them together in order, with the title page on top. Staple the pages together along the left-hand side.

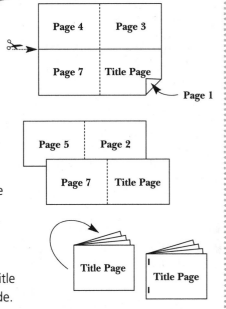

After Reading Encourage children to respond to what they've read by asking them what they liked most and least about the story. To assess their reading comprehension, ask children to do an oral retelling of the story.

Next, ask them to reflect on their experience reading the book. Where did they encounter problems and what did they do to solve them? Review parts of the text that children found challenging. Remind children to apply their knowledge of sound-spelling relationships when they get stuck on unfamiliar words. Also encourage them to use context clues in the text and pictures to figure out meanings.

You might also use this time to teach a mini-lesson on a particular phonics skill or to model good reading behaviors. For example, to demonstrate how punctuation affects your inflection, read aloud part of the text using somewhat exaggerated expression. Repeat the demonstration and then ask children to read aloud with you. If children have difficulty reading dialogue, demonstrate how to make the voices of each character distinct. Again, after you have read a sentence with expression, invite children to echo your reading.

You can help children build reading confidence by having them read each book several times. For more practice, children can pair up to read a book together and help each other with unfamiliar words. Again, tap into each child's progress by listening to individuals read aloud and by keeping notes.

Extending the Books

Connections to the Language Arts Standards

The activities in this book are designed to support you in meeting the following reading standards outlined by the Mid-continent Research for Education and Learning (McRel), an organization that collects and synthesizes national and state K–12 curriculum standards.

✳ Understands that print conveys meaning

✳ Understands how print is organized and read (e.g., identifies front and back covers, title pages, author, follows words from left-to-right and from top-to-bottom; knows the significance of spaces between words, knows the difference between letters, words, and sentences; understands the use of capitalization and punctuation as text boundaries)

✳ Creates mental images from pictures and print

✳ Uses basic elements of phonetic analysis to decode unknown words

✳ Understands level-appropriate sight words and vocabulary

✳ Uses self-correction strategies

✳ Reads aloud familiar stories with fluency and expression

Source—*Content Knowledge: A Compendium of Standards and Benchmarks for K–12 Education* (3rd ed.). (Mid-Continent Research for Education and Learning, 2000)

Little Reader Library Totes

Invite children to create their very own library totes for storing and carrying their little readers. Gather boxes sized about 6 to 7 inches wide, 4½ to 5 inches tall, and 2 to 3 inches deep. (Boxes containing packets of hot cereal or snack bars work well.) Then help children follow these steps to make their totes:

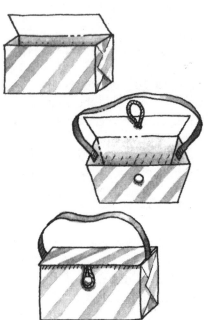

1. Securely tape any open flaps closed.

2. Use a glue stick to cover the outside of the box with gift wrap or craft paper.

3. Turn the box upside down. To make a hinged lid, make three cuts in the bottom of the box (now the top), as shown. (You can leave the side flaps on or cut them off.)

4. For a handle, staple a 12-inch piece of ribbon to the sides of the box, on the interior.

5. To make a closure, hot glue (adult only) a button or decorative bead to the front of the box, in the middle, as shown. Then affix a loop of ribbon or yarn to the underside of the lid, in the middle.

Children can decorate their totes using markers, stickers, and other craft materials.

Write a Little Reader

Using the language structure of different mini-books in the collection, children can try their hand at writing their very own books. For example, after children have read "What Is Red?" they might enjoy writing stories about other colors. On the chalkboard or chart paper, write another color word, such as *green*. Ask children to name things that are green. (*leaves, frogs, peas, grasshoppers*, and so on) Then write the sentence frame, _____ *are green. Green, green, green.* Provide children with white copy paper cut to quarter- or half-page size. On each page, have children copy and complete the sentence frame and draw a picture to illustrate it. Then have them write *What Is Green?* on a construction paper cover and staple the pages of their book together. Invite children to innovate on the text in other stories, as well, such as "What Do I Need?," "Almost Spring," and "Look What I Found!"

Sort and Read

To strengthen skills in critical thinking, reading comprehension, and interpreting context clues, have children practice sequencing the pages of some of the stories. Examples to try include "Hurry Up! Hurry Up!," "What Do I Need?," "Sweet Treat," "Cold Rose," and "I Can Draw!" Before

photocopying, mask the numbers on the mini-book pages. Then make single-sided copies, cut apart the mini-book pages, and give them to children, out of order. Ask children to put the pages of the book in order and then read the book to a friend. Encourage them to talk with each other about why certain pages come before and after others, and why, in some books, more than one sequence of the pages might be reasonable. After this discussion, children can make any needed adjustments, number the pages, and staple their book together.

Reading and Writing Activities Across the Curriculum

Following are additional ideas and activities for extending the themes covered in this collection. Each activity is based on a book from one of the five main themes.

SCHOOL DAYS

Playground Opposites Wheel (Reading and Writing)

The story "Fun at the Playground" (pages 23–24) gives children practice reading high-frequency sight words that are opposites. To reinforce the pairs of opposites in the story, have children make Playground Opposites Wheels.

1. Give each child copies of pages 9–10. Invite children to color the wheels and then cut them out. (For added durability, have them glue the pages to oaktag before cutting.)

2. Show children how to cut out the window and flap door along the dotted lines.

3. Model how to place the shape wheel on top of the word/picture wheel, align the center dots, push a brass fastener through the dots, and open to secure.

4. To use their wheel, children turn the bottom wheel so the words appear in the window. Encourage them to read each word before lifting the flap to see the picture.

FRIENDS, FRIENDS, FRIENDS

Make a Sweet Treat! (Art and Writing)

Invite children to make their own ice-cream sundaes after reading the story "Sweet Treat" (pages 33–34). To start, give each child a copy of page 11, a sheet of construction paper, crayons, scissors, and a glue stick. Have children color the pictures and cut them out. Encourage them to use their imagination to create different flavors of ice cream. Then, using the construction paper as a background, have them assemble the ice-cream sundae of their dreams! (Have extra copies of the pattern page on hand for adding extra scoops.) Afterward, encourage children to label the parts of their sundae using the words in their "Sweet Treat" book (along with your help) as a reference tool. Then invite children to take turns describing the delicious-looking sundaes they created.

WHAT'S IN MY WORLD?

What Can I See? Magnifier Books (Science and Writing)

After reading "What Can I See?" (pages 43–44), invite children to make pretend magnifiers to get a close-up look at the world outdoors.

1. Give each child a copy of page 12. Have children glue the page to oaktag, cut out the magnifier pattern along the outer and inner dotted lines, and color.

2. Take children outdoors to a local park to make observations and take notes. Give children clipboards, paper, and pencils so they can record their findings. (For easy-to-make clipboards, give each child a binder clip and a piece of cardboard.) Encourage children to hold their magnifiers to their eyes for a focused look at their surroundings.

3. Back in the classroom, provide children with extra copies of the magnifier page. Instead of cutting out the center of the magnifier, children can use this space to record some of the things they observed on their walk using the sentence frame "I see _____." They can also draw pictures of the things they saw.

4. Afterward, have children add a magnifier cover with the title "What Can [child's name] See?" To bind their book, have children stack the pages, punch a hole in the handles, and use a brass fastener to secure them. To read their book, children can fan out the magnifier pages, one by one.

AROUND THE SEASONS

Hibernating Puppet Pals (Reading and Drama)

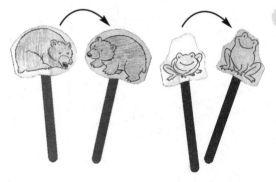

For a Reader's Theater version of "Winter Is Here" (pages 47–48), invite children to make puppets to dramatize the story during a rereading. Divide the class into groups of six and have each child choose the part of one of the animals. Give each group a copy of page 13 and have children color and cut out the two-sided animal patterns. Then direct them to fold the puppets in half and glue to a craft stick, as shown. As they read their page, have children show their animal going to sleep. When the group reaches the end of the story, tell children to gently "wake up" their animals as they read the last page together.

ALL ABOUT ME

I Can Draw a Clown! (Art and Writing)

After reading "I Can Draw!" (pages 55–56), give children a copy of page 14 and invite them to read and follow the illustrated directions to draw a clown just like the one in the story! Afterward, children can try writing their own set of directions for drawing other pictures and then exchange them with classmates.

Playground Opposites Wheel

top

9

Playground Opposites Wheel

bottom

My First Little Readers Scholastic Teaching Resources

Make a Sweet Treat!

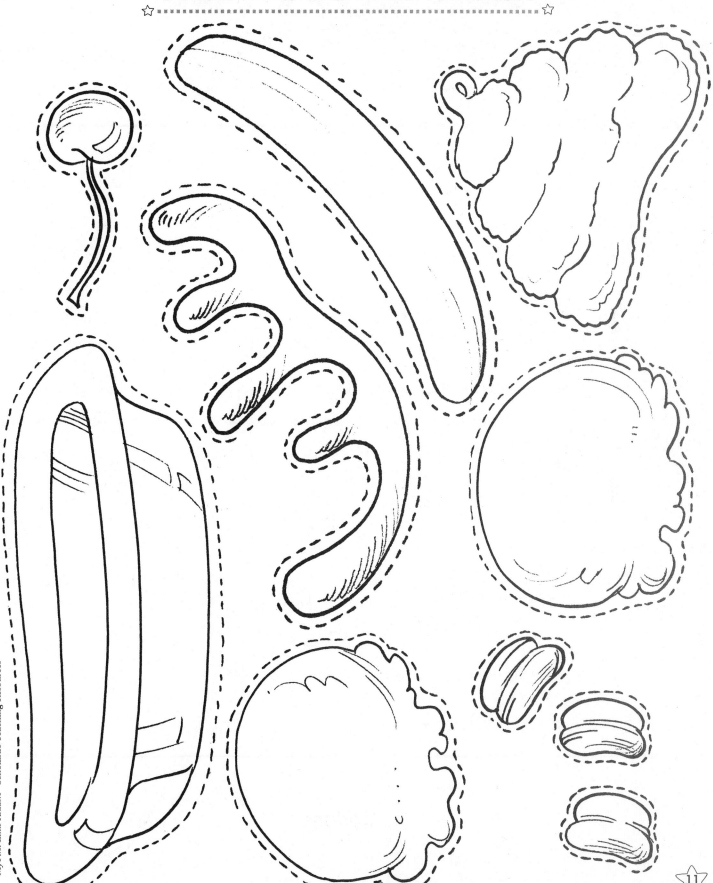

11

What Can I See? Magnifier Book

Hibernating Puppet Pals

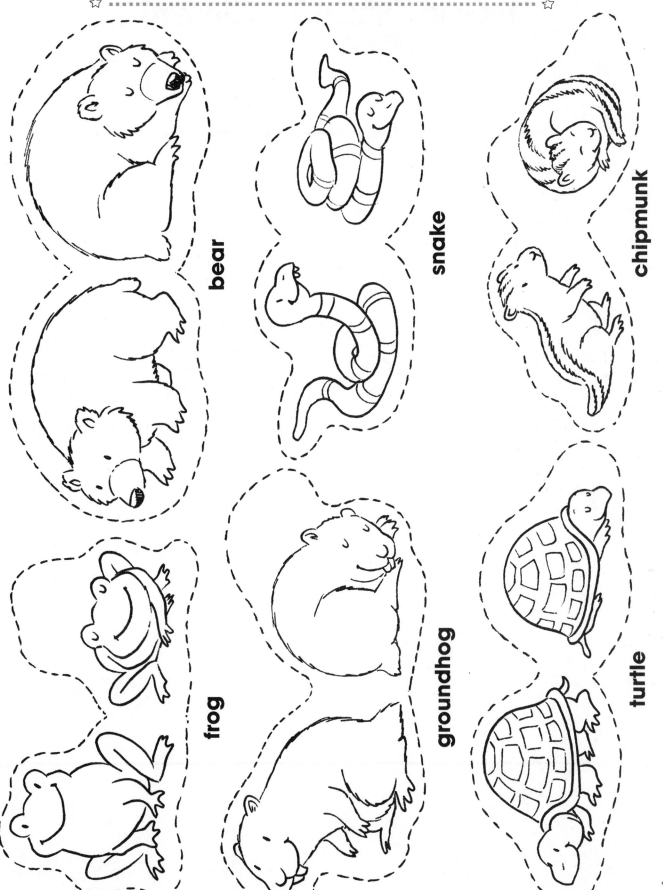

bear

snake

chipmunk

frog

groundhog

turtle

I Can Draw a Clown!

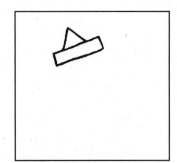

1. Draw a rectangle and a triangle for the hat.

2. Draw an oval for the head.

3. Draw a curved rectangle for the collar.

4. Draw 2 rectangles for arms.

5. Draw 2 lines for the shirt.

6. Draw 2 hands.

7. Draw hair and a face.

8. Draw 2 buttons!

3

Get dressed.
Hurry up! Hurry up!

My First Little Readers Scholastic Teaching Resources

Hurry Up! Hurry Up!

Eat breakfast.
Hurry up! Hurry up!

4

It is the first day of school!
Hurry up! Hurry up!

7

2

Brush my teeth.
Hurry up! Hurry up!

1

Get out of bed.
Hurry up! Hurry up!

5

Take my lunch.
Hurry up! Hurry up!

6

Get the bus.
Hurry up! Hurry up!

I like to cut.

My First Little Readers Scholastic Teaching Resources

I like to glue.

On a boat
I can sail.
The boat is
big and red.

I like school!

1

I like to read.

2

I like to paint.

My First Little Readers Scholastic Teaching Resources

I like to write.

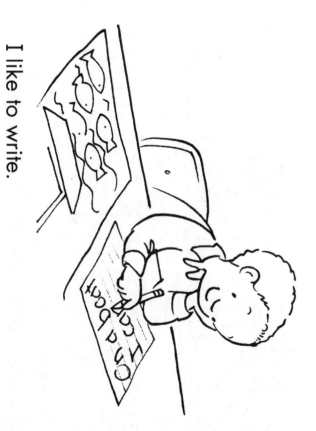

I like to count.

 6

 5

The mouse crawls
around and around.

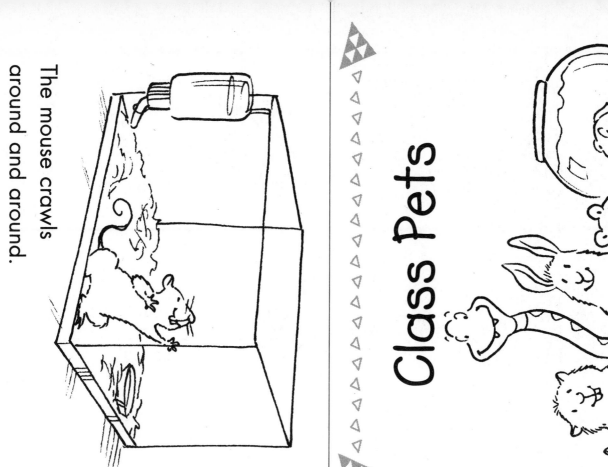

Class Pets

My First Little Readers Scholastic Teaching Resources

The hamster runs
around and around.

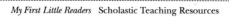

Class pets
all around and around!

The rabbit sniffs
around and around.

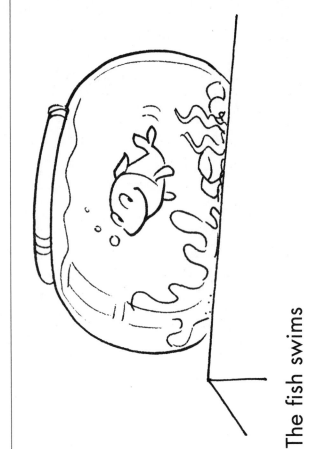

The fish swims
around and around.

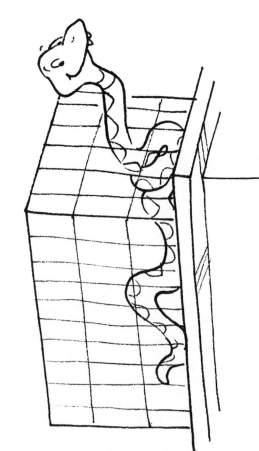

The snake slides
around and around.

The frog hops
around and around.

I like to eat an oval.

Shapes for Lunch

I like to eat a rectangle.

Shapes are fun
for lunch!

I like to eat a square.

I like to eat a triangle.

My First Little Readers Scholastic Teaching Resources

I like to eat a half-circle.

I like to eat a circle.

I go high.

Fun at the Playground

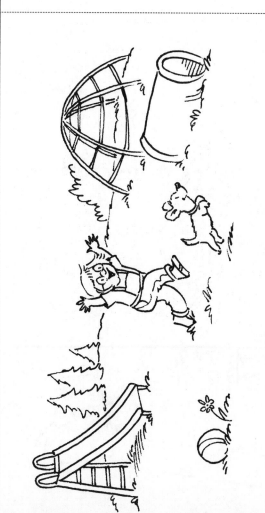

My First Little Readers Scholastic Teaching Resources

I go low.

At the playground,
I get around!

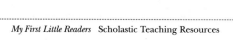

1

I go in.

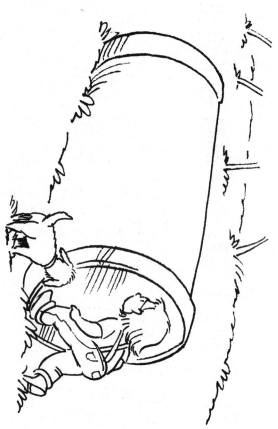

2

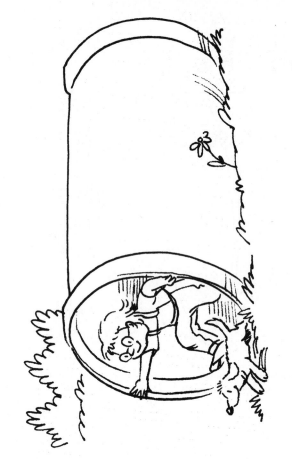

I go out.

6

I go down.

5

I go up.

I need a blanket.

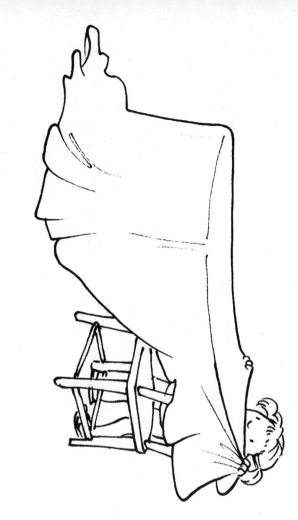

What Do I Need?

My First Little Readers Scholastic Teaching Resources

I need a pillow.

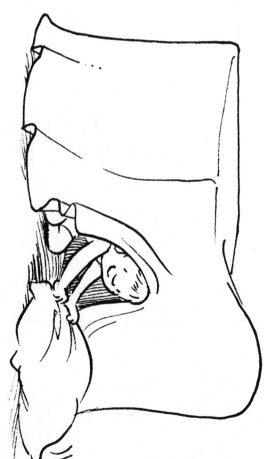

I need a friend!

I need a table.

I need a chair.

My First Little Readers Scholastic Teaching Resources

I need a flashlight.

I need a snack.

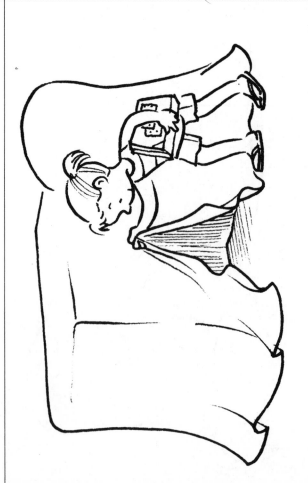

I have ribbon.

Birthday Surprise

I have a birthday card for you!

I have glue.

I have paper.

I have scissors.

I have crayons.

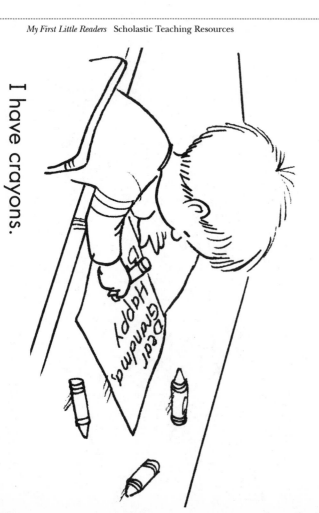

Dear Grandma,
Happy

I have stickers.

Mud pies.

Fun With Mud

Mud donuts.

Bake sale!

Mud cookies.

Mud cakes.

My First Little Readers Scholastic Teaching Resources

Mud bread.

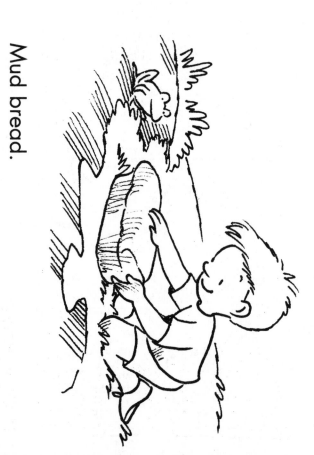

Mud muffins.

Where Is Petey?

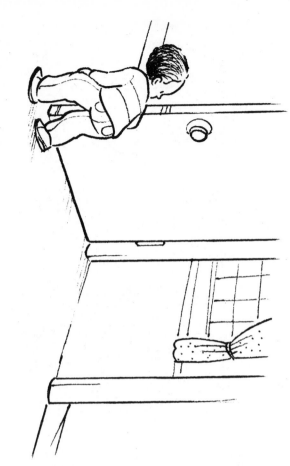

Is he behind the door?

My First Little Readers   Scholastic Teaching Resources

Is he in the drawer?

Here is Petey!

Where is Petey?
Is he under the bed?

Is he in the shed?

My First Little Readers Scholastic Teaching Resources

Is he under the rug?

Is he in the tub?

I add the chocolate.

Sweet Treat

You add the whipped cream.

We share dessert!

I add the banana.

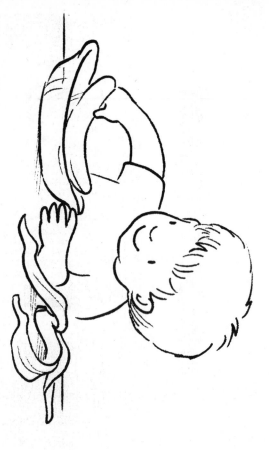

You add the ice cream.

Chocolate Ice Cream

Vanilla Ice Cream

You add the cherries.

Cherries

I add the nuts.

The moon shines.

What Shines?

My First Little Readers   Scholastic Teaching Resources

A dime shines.

I shine!

The sun shines.

A flashlight shines.

My shoes shine.

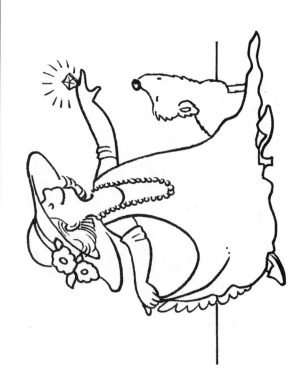

A ring shines.

3

A flag has stripes.
I like stripes.

I Like Stripes

My First Little Readers Scholastic Teaching Resources

4

A zebra has stripes.
I like stripes.

A ladybug has spots.
I like spots!

7

1

A candy cane has stripes.
I like stripes.

2

Toothpaste has stripes.
I like stripes.

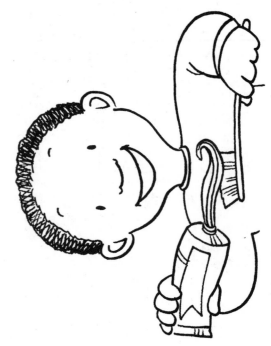

6

A ladybug has stripes.
No! No! No!

5

A street has stripes.
I like stripes.

Fire trucks are red.
Red, red, red.

What Is Red?

Stop signs are red.
Red, red, red.

My face is red.
Red, red, red!

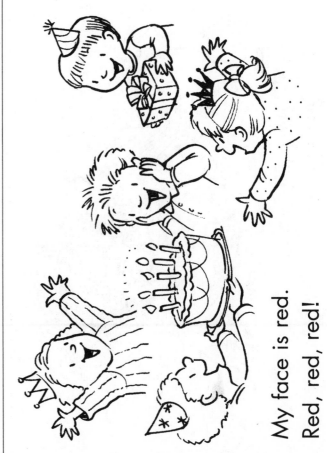

Apples are red.
Red, red, red.

Strawberries are red.
Red, red, red.

Hearts are red.
Red, red, red.

Flowers are red.
Red, red, red.

Bubbles in the sink.

Bubbles!

My First Little Readers Scholastic Teaching Resources

Bubbles in my drink.

Bubbles, bubbles, bubbles, everywhere I go!

Bubbles at the beach.

Bubbles in the bath.

Bubbles that I blow.

Bubbles in the clothes.

I see a leaf.

What Can I See?

My First Little Readers Scholastic Teaching Resources

I see a home.

But no one can see me!

2

I see a stone.

1

I see an ant.

5

I see a bee.

6

I see a flower.

Cold toes.
Cold Rose!

Cold Rose

My First Little Readers   Scholastic Teaching Resources

Warm clothes.

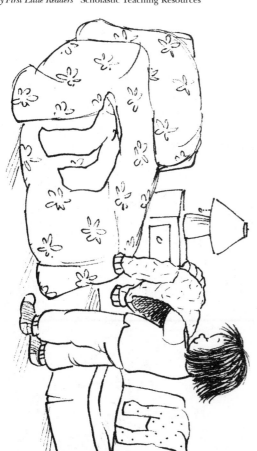

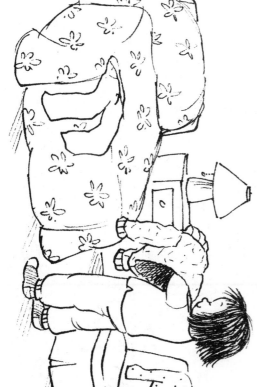

Warm Rose!

1

Cold clothes.

2

Cold nose.

6

Warm nose.

5

Warm toes.

Winter is here.
Sleep, chipmunk, sleep.

My First Little Readers Scholastic Teaching Resources

Winter Is Here

Spring is here.
Time to wake up!

Winter is here.
Sleep, frog, sleep.

1

Winter is here.
Sleep, bear, sleep.

Winter is here.
Sleep, snake, sleep.

Winter is here.
Sleep, groundhog, sleep.

6

Winter is here.
Sleep, turtle, sleep.

5

Birds are singing.
It is almost spring.

Almost Spring

My First Little Readers Scholastic Teaching Resources

Flowers are budding.
It is almost spring.

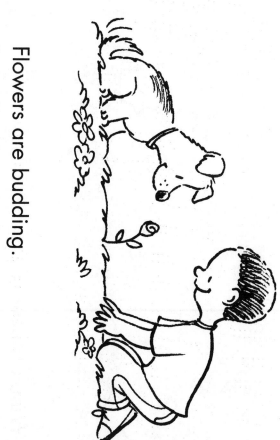

Spring is here!

1

Sun is shining.
It is almost spring.

2

Snow is melting.
It is almost spring.

My First Little Readers Scholastic Teaching Resources

6

Chicks are peeping.
It is almost spring.

5

Wind is blowing.
It is almost spring.

When night comes,
the moth comes out.

When Night Comes

When night comes,
the bat comes out.

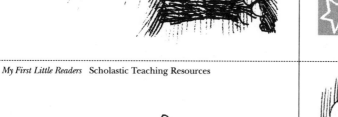

When night comes,
I go inside!

2

When night comes,
the owl comes out.

1

When night comes,
the mouse comes out.

5

When night comes,
the firefly comes out.

6

When night comes,
the cat comes out.

Hello, shell.

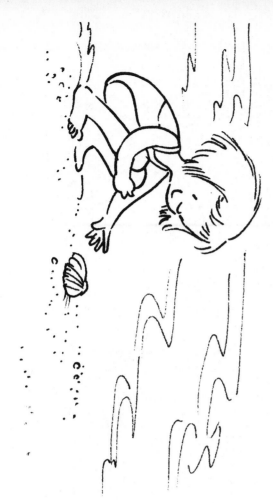

Hello, Beach

Hello, crab.

Well, hello, WHALE!

Hello, sun.

Hello, sand.

Hello, sail.

Hello, gull.

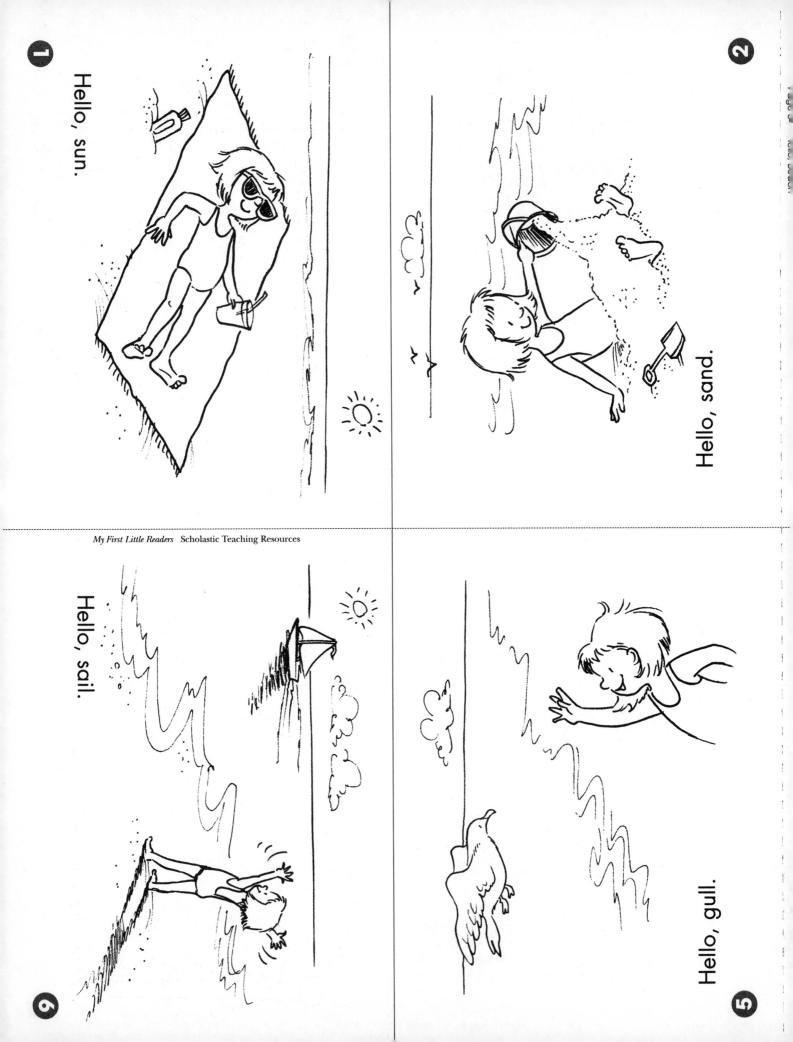

3

I can draw a king.

I Can Draw!

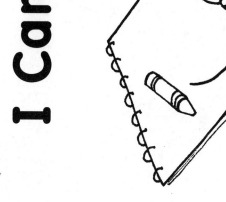

4

I can draw a crown.

7

I can draw myself to sleep.

z-z-z-z

1

I can draw a seal.

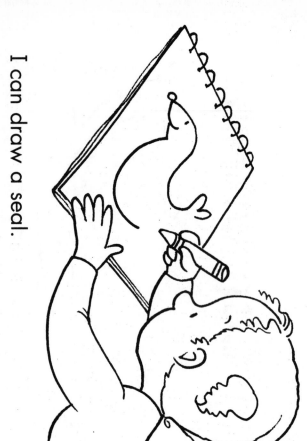

2

I can draw a clown.

My First Little Readers Scholastic Teaching Resources

6

I can draw a bed.

5

I can draw a sheep.

I can hide behind my hair.

Hide and Seek

My First Little Readers   Scholastic Teaching Resources

I can hide in a dress.

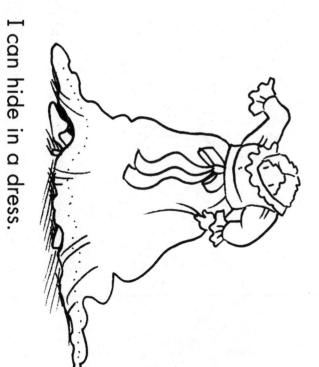

I can hide in a hug!

1

Where can I hide?

2

I can hide behind a chair.

6

I can hide under the rug.

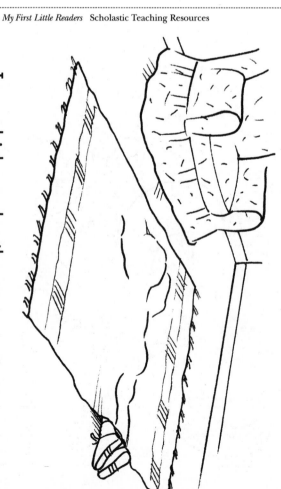

5

I can hide in a mess.

I have a hat that has holes.

Hats, Hats, Hats

I have a hat that rolls.

Hats, hats, hats.
I like hats a lot!

I have a hat that is tall.

I have a hat that is small.

My First Little Readers Scholastic Teaching Resources

I have a hat that is a mop.

I have a hat that flops.

I like tacos.

What Is for Supper?

My First Little Readers Scholastic Teaching Resources

I like grilled cheese.

I like to eat!

1

I like pasta.

2

I like pizza.

6

I like rice and beans.

5

I like fish sticks.

3

I found an acorn.

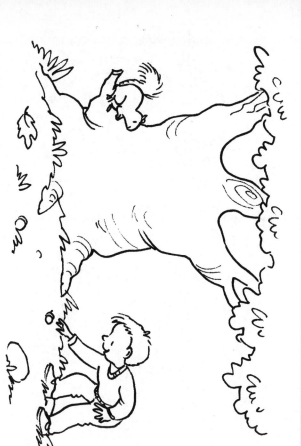

Look What I Found!

My First Little Readers Scholastic Teaching Resources

4

I found a pine cone.

7

I found six things all together!

Look what I found!
I found a stick.

I found a stone.

My First Little Readers Scholastic Teaching Resources

I found a feather.

I found a leaf.